# The Insect Hotel

## David Stringer

### foreword by Bill Oddie OBE

# Dedication

For Harry, who inspired this book

# Foreword by Bill Oddie

How many times have you been reading a bedtime story to your child or children whilst thinking to yourself: "I could do better than this!?" Lots of parents do, judging from how many letters, synopses, manuscripts and even what appear to be finished books I get sent. Some are OK. Most definitely aren't! I usually write back, trying to be complimentary without being too encouraging. The fact is that, even if the book is fabulous, there isn't much I can do about it. I am not a publisher! I don't even hang out in literary society, which tends to involve a lot of liquid lunches (and suppers, and even the odd breakfast).

In fact, David Stringer contacted me by E Mail, sent via my agent (enterprising) including a concise CV (not too long), several pages (but not too many) of the manuscript of The Insect Hotel, plus a polite (but not obsequious) request for me to provide a forward. David even added a couple lines of compliments about my work, past and present - from comedy to wildlife- but this is not what impressed me. Honest.

What I immediately took to was the writing. The words, the language, the dialogue. Unlike many children's books about wildlife —and there are many – it is not patronising or over simplistic. The text is instantly – and I can't think of a more appro-

priate word - "natural". It conjures up scenes and scenarios, and captures the relationship and conversation between a father and son. It is unavoidably "educational", as is anything that deals with adventures and discoveries. As too is humour. Laughter teaches us what we enjoy. I confidently predict that you will enjoy reading The Insect Hotel, and if you think "I could do better than this", I bet you can't. If you can, find a publisher!

By the way, I am assuming that young children don't read book Forwards. This bit is for the grownups.

BILL ODDIE

August 2013.

# Preface

This book is based on some fun short stories my four year old son Harry and I came up with, for bed times, as I not only tried to settle him down for the night but also to add a little fun to our newly found discoveries in the garden.

This originally started out as a little, cost-effective activity we did together as we built, from scraps of materials found in our garden and shed, a little 'Insect Hotel' designed to encourage insects and other wildlife into our garden, as well as help get us both out of the house for some much needed fresh air, physical activity and fun.

A picture of our 'Insect Hotel' can be found on our website, www.theinsecthotel.com. I'm sure you'll be impressed. (Hm-mmm?) We would love you to visit us there, get in touch and maybe even share with us your garden discoveries or Insect Hotels!

Anyway, I hope you enjoy reading about some of the adventures we've had and some of the new friends we've had visit us.

Thank you.

David & Harry

# Contents

# 1: Woodster

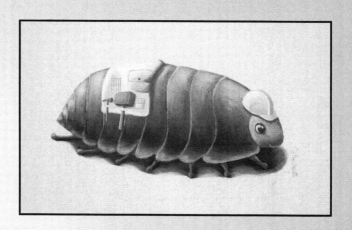

It was a lovely, sunny summer's day. The garden was an explosion of green, which was well overdue some attention. Likewise Harry was well overdue some fresh air, fun and more importantly, some distraction from wearing his dad out.

"Where to start," thought Dad, looking around the garden.

The grass as usual was growing fast and needed another trim. A few weeds were starting to raise their unwanted heads mockingly around various corners of the garden and more than one bush could do with a haircut.

"I know," thought Dad, looking to delay the inevitable work that awaited him, "I'll check on the strawberries and rhubarb, and see how the Insect Hotel is holding up."

Once the fruit was checked (and looking good, if he did say so himself!) Dad walked over to see the 'Insect Hotel'. At this stage of development the Hotel wasn't quite complete. It had two floors, walls, doors, interior decorations and soft furnishings (leaves, straw, sticks and bamboo) but lacked something.

Harry wandered over, munching on a cheese and ham sandwich.

"Can I help, Dad?" he said, words that Dad knew meant any job would now take a little longer than usual.

"Course you can, buddy. Just looking at our Insect Hotel... think it needs something."

Harry stared over at the rather sad looking heap of wood and brick.

"More floors?" Harry suggested helpfully.

"Love to, but we've not got any more bricks," grumbled Dad.

Harry went thoughtful for a moment, still munching on his sandwich.

"Helicopter pad?" he said, eyes wide.

"Not quite what I had in mind." Dad smiled. "But I like the idea."

With that, Dad wandered off into the shed, while Harry swallowed the last of the sandwich and slowly followed behind wondering what his old man was up to.

Inside the shed, holding and considering small pieces of wood Dad asked, "How about we bang some old nails into these and try to build a roof?" He smiled to himself proudly.

Harry replied with an excited, "Yeah!" while reaching up and trying to prise the hammer from his Dad's hand.

Later that night, Harry was still rolling around in his duvet, delaying the bedtime that was quickly approaching, and burning the last bit of endless energy he always had when he knew he'd soon have to go to sleep. Suddenly he stopped and shouted, "Oh no! We didn't finish the roof for the hotel." He looked at Dad with his bottom lip starting to wobble, concern splashed all over his face.

Panicking and weary, realising this occurrence would seriously delay bedtime, Dad quickly said, "Of course we did!"

"We didn't, we didn't finish the roof. Let's go do it now." Harry jumped up and started to clamber off his bed.

"Oh, no you don't," Dad spluttered as he quickly scooped up a wriggly Harry and placed him back into bed while trying at the same time to drag the duvet back into position.

"It's bedtime, you're in your pyjamas and... erm... Woodster's doing it!"

Harry paused. "Who?"

Woodster was a woodlouse who had lived in the garden for quite some time, in insect years. He was grey in colour, stubborn and was one of the finest 'Handy Bugs' around. Although it should be noted he didn't like being referred to as a 'Handy Bug' as he considered himself more of a crab than a bug, being all strong and having a tough, scaly shield-like back. But he'd decided to let the matter drop long ago, as it did help bring work in (being referred to as a bug) with other insects in the garden and on top of that, his business cards had already been printed.

He looked the Insect Hotel construction site over. Huge cranes made from reeds towered over the rubble-filled building site, helping load or move stones and debris about as little ants and gnats flittered about looking dust-covered and busy, without a lot seeming to change.

"A roof, he says," muttered Woodster to himself while scratching his head. "Surely a helicopter pad would be better?"

With that he ventured off towards the shed while juggling from one leg to the other a little ratchet.

"Told you, Dad," pointed out Harry smugly.

"Hey, what do I know?" shrugged Dad.

Hammer in hand, Woodster starting bashing nails into the large piece of wood that would soon become the Insect Hotel's new roof.

"Stop!" he suddenly yelled, dropping the piece of wood and hammer he was holding and rushing over to the other side of the gigantic plank of material, which was currently surrounded by a handful of now startled-looking ants. "What do you think you are doing?"

The huddled group of ants had now frozen still, as if part of a picture, daring not to move or breathe. All of them, wide-eyed and open-mouthed, with their ill fitting red hard hats all seemingly worn at an angle on their little heads, stared nervously at the approaching and angry looking woodlouse.

"This is my job, my responsibility, not yours!" Woodster continued. "If this goes wrong, it's me that gets the flak."

He had reached them now and being slightly bigger, found himself staring down at them curiously. All five of them looked identical in every way, he noticed, with a slight smile to himself, even that they were all covered in mud, dust and dew in exactly the same way. How did they manage that?

"Off you pop, lads. My job, and I don't want any help." And with that, he raised one of his arms and pointed at the garden, indicating the direction of their departure, similar to that of an air stewardess showing passengers where the doors are for dis-embarkment.

The confused group of ants, all looking at each other while scratching their heads and adjusting their hard hats, slowly start-ed to walk away. Then one of them stopped, looked the gigantic plank up and down, and looked back at Woodster with a frown. Looking down at the ground, he nervously replied in a high pitched squeaky voice, "Are you sure? Looks a mighty big job for one."

"Not for me, it's not," said Woodster.

The banging noise of hammer on nail bounced around the garden repeatedly for days, almost like the regular tick tocking of a big clock, which was now starting to annoy more than the odd occupant of the garden.

Woodster, with hard hat now on the floor and replaced with a banana bandana (which interestingly was made from a banana skin), was covered head to toes in sweat and looking very hot and bothered. If it's possible for a woodlouse to get sun burnt Woodster surely was, not that he'd admit it, mind.

"How's it going?" yelled an inquisitive and helpful worker ant, red hard hat in hand.

"Fine!"

The ant looked the wooden plank up and down. It seemed to stretch almost as far as he could see. "Sure you don't want any help?"

"Sure!" snapped Woodster, who hadn't stopped hammering away or looked up at the worker ant.

"Okay," grumbled the ant disappointedly as he turned to leave the work site. Cranes were still standing tall and proud in the hot sunshine, wind slowly blowing bits of dust up into the air and over huge piles of slowly baking metal nails that lay in waiting for action. As he departed and under his breath he muttered to himself, "What a plank."

A few days later, with the grumbles of the hotel management still ringing in his ears about the amount of time being taken to complete the job and the noise that he was making which was upsetting the locals, Woodster wiped his sweaty brow with his now black and wilted looking banana bandana as he looked the huge wooden roof up and down.

It was now nearly half complete, with one of the triangle shaped sides firmly attached to the bigger plank, which would become the roof. He just needed to attach another triangle shaped piece of wood to the other side of the big plank and then a smaller back panel to keep it all secure. With a sinking feeling, he said to himself, "Nope, not quite halfway."

He then wearily started to climb up one of the cranes, made from reeds, hammer in hand. "Can't wait to get this job done," he thought.

"Bang, bang, bang," came the familiar, but now less energetic, sound to all in the garden as Woodster continued his apparently never-ending task. His mind started to wander. He imagined how nice it would be to if he were drinking a nice, cool glass of 'sip of sap' on the luxurious and peaceful balconies of the blossom tree when suddenly, Whack!

"Aaagggghhhhh," he yelled in pain as his hammer came crashing down on one of his hands, rather than a metal nail. He lost his balance on top of the crane as he tensed up in agony, and then suddenly could feel himself drifting backwards. He quickly scrunched up his hard, shell like back as he prepared for the inevitable... THUMP of the ground.

Woodster slowly lifted his heavy eyelids. His vision was all blurred as if he were looking through water. His head was thumping as if someone had parked a hammer into it and he could still feel an ache in his hand like a nagging mum moaning at you to finish your greens.

"Uuuurrrghhhh," he groaned in an attempt at speech.

Then as his view slowly started to clear, the fogginess started to move. He could make out a few strange little faces peering at him, all wearing red hard hats as well as concerns across their faces. It was those pesky worker ants again, he realised.

"Won't they just leave me alone?" he thought. He started to try and get up to shoo them away, when, as he leaned forward, his knees suddenly buckled and he fell backwards again.

"Easy, grumpy fella," said one of the little faces.

"You've had a huge fall."

"And bump!" jumped in one of the little voices.

"Uuuurrrghhhh," groaned Woodster again, stroking his sore head while trying to take in what had happened.

"Come on, lads!" said what appeared to be the lead ant, as they all swarmed round him and carefully lifted him up.

"Time for some rest," squeaked one of the little voices, and with that they quickly carried him away while he was still too weak to resist, or argue back.

"Rest for the garden," giggled one of the ants, "from that constant and annoying hammering".

"I could get used to this," thought Woodster as he lazed around in the comfort of one of the hotel's rooms. It had been a few days since his fall and wallop at the building site, and he was now pretty much fully recovered. At first he fretted about the completion of the roof and tried to rush back to work, but lack of energy and the determination of the hotel staff that he rest properly soon stopped that.

There was then a little tap at the door, which slowly opened. A little worker ant's head peered around it and into view.

"Morning," squeaked the ant.

"Morning, you. How's things?" replied Woodster in a friendly tone which completely surprised the worker ant who stammered back, "F-f-fine."

"Good stuff, now get over here and help me up. It's time that roof got completed."

The ant slowly walked over, looking around the room as if he expected something or someone to jump out at him.

"What is it?" asked Woodster.

The ant froze.

"Well?"

"It's just that..." the ant stammered awkwardly

"What?" cried out Woodster, now losing his patience as various aches and pains started to return to his hand and head.

"We thought it would be nice if we, well, helped you."

Woodster stared at the ant. He knew what was coming.

"We have continued the construction of the roof using the giant plank."

Woodster slumped back into his bed of straw with a feeling of despair. "Oh great, back to square one."

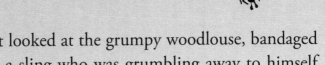

The worker ant looked at the grumpy woodlouse, bandaged head and hand in a sling who was grumbling away to himself with a confused look. "Square one?" he pondered.

Woodster then slowly started to pull himself up. "Right, better check on the new demolition site, hadn't we?"

The worker ants ran around, with their newly polished red hard hats and gleaming 'like new' work tools in a mixture of nerves and excitement, as if a member of the royal family was to visit.

Woodster arrived at the construction site with a slight feeling of anxiousness, where he had laboured for days on the newly ordered hotel roof. The huge cranes still stood tall, almost at attention, he thought. Piles of nails still sat around in smaller piles than before while a few gnats flitted about in the air making the place seem more active than it really was.

He almost let out a big sigh of relief, as he looked around noting the place wasn't as much of a disaster as he had feared! In fact, the place seemed to be ticking along almost nicely. "This can't be right," he thought with his usual suspicious mind.

He scanned around, trying to find something that must be amiss, something that surely was going to annoy him and cause him extra work and grief, something which would surely bug the heck out of him. But alas, there didn't appear to be anything. One of the worker ants, the lead one he suspected, came over with a big smile.

"Hi there, feeling okay?"

"Think so," replied Woodster, still looking around, almost disappointed that there was nothing wrong.

"Hope you don't mind too much. Know it's your job, but we thought we'd help out a little in your absence," the ant nervously spat out while pointing over to the huge plank of wood.

Woodster wandered over. The roof construction was almost complete, with both triangle sides now attached to the main roof section, with only the back panel needing more nails added.

Woodster suddenly stopped, picked up his old hard hat which was still lying on the floor, and placed it firmly back on his head. "Should always wear your safety gear, lads," he said out loud to no-one in particular, but secretly to himself. The fall wouldn't have hurt so much should he have kept it on, rather than the cooler and more comfortable banana bandana which did nothing to stop the bump on his head hurting.

"Good work, lads," he admitted.

The ants breathed a sigh of relief in unison.

"Looks like the job will get done in time now after all," he again said to no-one in particular, with what some of the ants thought looked like a smile. Woodster would, of course, deny this.

"Right then, boys, stop gawping at me and get started on that back panel," he barked, as all the ants suddenly jumped up happily and ran over to the back panel, tools in hand with a little work song breaking out into the air.

*Hi Ho, Hi Ho, it's off to work we go.*

Woodster smiled, turned around and found one of the ants, the lead one he thought, still stood there. "You okay, little fella?" he asked.

"I was thinking, erm, what if we... erm."

"Yes?"

"Well, what if we, well, erm..."

"Yes?" Woodster now replied in a more annoyed tone.

"Drilled some holes in the back panel?" the ant spluttered while making a drill motion with his hands and smiling.

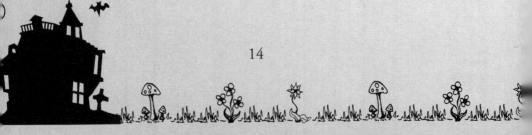

"Ha Ha," laughed out Harry, "That's what I did, too!"

Dad grinned.

Woodster, frown streaked across his face in a puzzled look at the ant, asked, "Why on earth would we want to do that?"

"Air Conditioning and solar powered lighting," beamed the ant.

Woodster paused for a moment, before laughing out loud. "BrilliANT!"

"And that, Harry, proves how help from friends, with team work, makes light of big jobs," Dad said in a bit of a hushed voice.

"And to be careful when climbing a crane made from reeds which are floppy," replied Harry knowingly.

Dad laughed out, "Oh, so true, Harry, so true!"

# 2: Stinker

Harry came flying out of the back door into the garden and blazing sunshine like a bullet shot from a gun, with Dad slowly trundling behind him with a big bag of rubbish balanced in between his arms heading uneasily towards the dustbin.

"Dad, what's this?" called out Harry. Something had caught his eye on his big, bright yellow slide as he cautiously got closer for some further investigation.

Dad, after feeding the dustbin the rubbish bag, wandered over to see what discovery Harry had made. Was it a dropped crisp packet, a lonely and lost sock or a discarded lolly pop stick, he wondered.

"Wow," said Dad in surprised amazement at not only finding something which didn't need picking up and returning to the dustbin, but was also something he hadn't seen for quite some time. Perched nervously on Harry's slide was a lovely light green coloured, flat and shield shaped bug.

"This, Harry, is what's known as a Green Shield Bug. Isn't it lovely?" Harry wasn't so sure he'd call it lovely, as he carefully looked it over with a wrinkled up nose.

"A what? What is it?"

"It's a Green Shield Bug, just look at the beautiful green colouring it has on its back," said Dad enthusiastically as he slowly reached out with a small piece of wood to encourage the bug to step onto it.

"There's nothing to worry about Harry, he's quite harmless although I think he's played quite enough on your slide for one day." Dad started walking slowly towards the back of the garden, carefully balancing Harry's new discovery on the piece of wood.

"What you doing, Dad?" quizzed Harry, following slowly behind.

"I'm taking our friend here back to the Insect Hotel. I think he still needs his rest."

"Cool!" cried out Harry, excited that the hotel was not only getting another guest, that Dad liked his new discovery but also a little bit secretly pleased that he was getting his slide back.

Later that night, as the daylight slowly passed behind the fencing and Harry started slowly settling down for bed, he asked, "Dad, that green bug we found, what was his name again and what does he do?"

"Well," Dad started. "He's a Green Shield Bug and the one we found today is known as 'Stinker'."

"Stinker," giggled Harry.

"Yep," smiled Dad, "and this is his story."

Stinker was getting a little tired. The sun beating down on him was making flying a tough task today as well as making him a little thirsty, but he knew he still had a few more items to sell so had to keep going. No rest for the little.

Stinker, you see, was the best bow tie sales bug this side of the bog.

19

It was then that he noticed the beautiful pink blossom tree from our garden and he said to himself, "Mmmmmm, time for a quick sip of sap," and darted down into our garden licking his now dry lips.

(Narrator's note: Sip of sap is to be said fast, and sounds more like zip of zap!)

While he guzzled down the much needed sip of sap from the tree, all relaxed and taking in the views, he saw a very interesting but odd looking building, tucked away peacefully behind some huge grasses, surrounded by various little bugs darting this way and that all looking very happy and contented.

"What's this?" he thought.

So he put down the now finished cup of sap, wiped his mouth and adjusted his tie as he slowly floated down for a closer look.

"Might be some bugs here in urgent need of a bow tie," he said to himself with a smile.

This is how Stinker first came across and discovered the wondrous 'Insect Hotel'.

"Just the two nights, please," Stinker informed the reception desk porter.

"And I'll order the rhubarb and runner bean trifle for lunch, if that's okay?" he yelled as he headed back towards the front door and out into the lovely warm sunshine.

Once outside Stinker stopped, looked around at the views of the garden from the hotel lobby, taking in the almost hypnotic dancing of the pink blossom tree branches caught in the gentle breeze, the fierce dark purple coloured wild flowers rocking gently, all tall and proud as well as the splendid looking ferns all ancient and majestically deep in thought.

"Right, who's ready for a new look," he said out loud, still scanning the area, then off he pounced, little suitcase in hand, looking for some insects to sell his wares to.

The first insect he came across was one of the ground staff worms, who had just raised his head out of the mud (well at least we hope it was his head!). "Good day, kind sir, how are we today?" Stinker asked, full of politeness and smiles.

"Ugh?" grunted the worm.

21

"You're looking well, clearly a hard working young chap. I do hope and assume you're appreciated and noticed around here by the bosses for your endless hard work," he continued, emphasising the word 'noticed' in his statement.

"Ugh?" grunted the worm.

"Fear not, young worm. I have just the ticket to make you stand out and get noticed by your bosses! This will all but guarantee a pay rise in your next collection of crumbs." And with that Stinker eagerly opened up and dived into his suitcase, rummaging through what appeared to the worm an endless pit of bow ties.

"Got ya!" shrieked Stinker with delight, as he jumped out of the dark green, and slightly battered suitcase holding aloft a huge brown bow tie with the image of a spade on it.

"Ugh?" grunted the worm as he was passed the bow tie.

"All yours for just a chocolate cookie crumb," winked Stinker.

And this was how the rest of the day continued, with Stinker finding unsuspecting garden insects to push onto his luxurious, all weather wearing, top of the range bow ties.

"So why is he called Stinker?" asked Harry.

"I'm coming to that bit."

Harry grinned.

The next morning Stinker left his crumb filled hotel room, suitcase in hand, all upbeat and raring to go for more friendly banter and sales. He wiped the last of the rhubarb and runner bean trifle from his lips, plus the bits which had dropped down onto his top and whizzed off out into the great big garden yonder.

"Good day to you kind sirs," he remarked as he came across a couple of house sparrows.

They both turned to him, suddenly looking more menacing than before, with their dark piercing black eyes, their sharp short 'no nonsense' beaks and sturdy looking greyish-brown breast and cheeks.

"What we got here then," squawked one of the sparrows.

"Looks like a hand delivered take away lunch to me," replied the other, and with that they both as quick as a flash jumped up and surrounded poor Stinker.

Stinker froze in fear.

"Nothing to say before we all have lunch together?" giggled one of the sparrows

Stinker instinctively raised his suitcase up as a kind of shield or safety blanket.

"What's that?" asked the bigger sparrow.

"Nothing. I mean, well, it's my suitcase."

The sparrows both tilted their heads, looking at the case with curiosity. "Can we eat it?"

"Not really, it's a case, full of bow ties! Don't suppose either of you are interested in a bow tie?" Stinker stammered nervously, his stomach now churning as panic set in a little.

Both sparrows laughed. "Nuts maybe, or worms, but no, not interested in bow ties."

"Just food," boomed the other sparrow, moving in close now to Stinker.

Suddenly a strange noise came from behind Stinker somewhere, making all three of them jump a little and look curiously behind Stinker.

"What was that?" asked Stinker.

"No idea, sounded like thunder escaping from a small trumpet," said one of the hungry birds.

Stinker was too afraid to look behind him. Whatever the noise was, it felt close. Almost like a smack on the bum.

"Anyway, where was we?"

"About to eat some take away green bug," recalled one of them, who as he moved closer suddenly threw his head back.

"What the......" he shrieked in disgust, covering his beak with his wing.

"What?" both the remaining sparrow and Stinker asked at the same time.

The nose covered sparrow hopped away, almost dizzy with drowsiness from the fumes which had hit his nose and were now blasting the back of his head.

"Blah!" he yelled. "That is disgusting."

"What is?" the other sparrow asked with concern

"Him," replied the aroma victim, pointing his spare wing at Stinker.

"He's rotten or something." And with that he jumped up and flew away, coughing as he did so. The other sparrow looked at the nervous looking Green Bug, shook his head disapprovingly, and followed his friend away up into the air.

"Phew," sighed Stinker with relief, then turning around and sniffing gently said out loud again, "Phew!"

Back in the hotel lobby, both Stinker and a friendly wood-louse bug he had just met (Woodster) laughed and giggled together at the retelling of the Green Shield Bug's recent tale, while downing a few sips of sap.

"That was close," chuckled Woodster, patting the green bug on the back.

"Deary me. Talk about runner bean juice running to the rescue," giggled Stinker, as they both laughed amongst themselves for the rest of the dwindling evening.

"So he trumped on them," laughed Harry.

"Kind of. When nervous that's how Stinker protects himself," grinned Dad.

Harry continued to giggle and then practise his own form of Stinker protection, while Dad tried to regain calm, ready for lights out.

"Probably not the best subject material to calm you down for bed," shrugged Dad.

# 3: Curly Whirly

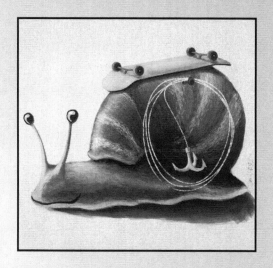

Dad was just putting the last of the grass cuttings into his composter when he realised Harry hadn't helped (hindered?) him for a few minutes. Looking around, he spotted Harry who was sat quietly and contentedly, legs crossed on the grass examining something in his hands.

"What you got there, trouble?" Dad asked as he wandered over.

"Snail, Dad," was the reply. "Calling him Curly Whirly."

"Sounds good, can I have a look?"

Harry put his hand out, showing Dad the snail which was sitting happily in the palm of his hand, or at least he was doing a good impression of a snail being happy, while in a little boy's sticky hand.

"Calling him Curly Whirly as he's got chocolate brown lines on him, which go round and round," said Harry proudly.

Dad smiled. "Good idea, kidder. Hope your being gentle with him!"

Harry just looked at Dad.

"Right, it's time to water some of the plants. That's your job, Harry!" Dad reminded him. "Let's put the snail, I mean Curly Whirly, somewhere safe." And with that, Dad started to walk off towards the house. Harry jumped up, looked around the garden and then with a beaming smile headed towards the Insect Hotel.

Carefully putting the snail down near the reception area, Harry quietly whispered, "See you later, Curly," and bounded off towards the house to get his watering can.

No rest for the little.

As Dad finished off reading the last page of Harry's bedtime book, Harry sat up. "Dad, tell me about Curly Whirly!"

Dad quietly groaned, his eyes rolling to the back of his head, foolishly thinking his bedtime task was done. "Well, what did Curly tell you? You two seemed to be having a good chat."

Harry smiled. "Well…" He paused for a moment as he stared into nothing with what clearly seemed to be a thousand thoughts crashing around his mind. "He told me his name and that he liked chocolate."

Curly Whirly was a young, energetic and carefree snail. He loved the outdoors, having a good explore and meeting new bugs, but his main passion, well, that was thrill seeking!

Curly Whirly's favourite activities included web jumping, rock sliming and shellblading of which he was the garden's current world champion!

Today Curly Whirly was practising for a big, garden wide shellblading race. His shell was nicely cleaned, waxed and polished with his chocolate coloured 'go faster' stripes shimmering in the bright sunlight.

He was feeling very proud of himself, looking at his reflection wearing his new designer 'Hugo Buzz' sunglasses and sundew sweet looking 'Red Bullfrog' racing helmet, when in the corner of his eye he spotted his old foe, Escargot.

Escargot was much bigger than Curly Whirly. He always hung around the pond area and had a very impressive brown pointy shaped shell, which he proudly told everyone made him more aerodynamic for racing. Much better then Curly Whirly's blunt, round shaped shell.

"Well, well, well," muttered Escargot in spotting Curly Whirly fitting his racing helmet. "You're surely not going to try and take me on again, are you?" he asked in a very arrogant tone.

"Of course," replied Curly Whirly, straining his neck to look up at his huge arch rival.

"Oh good!" Escargot said with relish as he leaned his head downwards towards his smaller and somewhat frustrating opponent, who somehow over the years always managed to beat him in shellblading races. And with that Curly Whirly gave Escargot a wink, and made his way to the top of the rubble pile ready to attempt his first practise run.

"Think it's time the pond tide turned," Escargot said out loud to himself in a menacing manner.

Things were going well in training for Curly Whirly. His time trials where good, his shell was looking good and his confidence was overflowing like lemonade in a glass being poured by Harry in the kitchen.

"How long to the race Curly?" enquired Stinker.

"Few more days."

"Hear the course is looking good, especially with all the different coloured wild flowers near the second turn," Stinker continued. "Think I might have a bow tie that would go with them."

"Yeah," replied Curly Whirly, not really listening. "Like I have time to look at flowers when racing at these speeds," he thought while adjusting his sunglasses, and with that off he popped towards the track.

Curly Whirly had got himself more distracted than normal for this race, as that huge and horrible Escargot seemed to be stepping up a gear (literally) somehow and was managing to pull in quicker race times than he was.

While lost in his own thoughts, Curly Whirly crossed paths with a few of the hotel worker ants, still wearing their little red hard hats. "Good luck this weekend, Curly!" they cheered.

"Yeah, thanks," he answered, again not really listening and again not stopping to talk with them.

"See if you can spot some lovely looking mushrooms growing near the last bend," a little ant called out, his voice becoming distant as the snail continued to ignore him and continued to venture towards the track.

Then in the distance he could hear a big cheer coming from the track. He picked up his pace to see what the carry on was, and get a closer look. His heart sunk when he reached the gate around the track and saw Escargot at the finishing line surrounded by lots of other insects, all a lot smaller than the huge snail, and all cheering and patting him on the shell.

He'd clearly got another good time. "Right," breathed Curly Whirly, firmly securing his helmet to his head and rushing down as fast as he could to the starting line for some more serious practising.

With only a few days until the race Curly Whirly wasn't looking his normal self. Normally he was happy-go-lucky, carefree and looking like he was on top of the world. The thrill of the race, his flash designer gear and the feel of the wind in his hair and tentacled eyes used to not only give the speedy snail a buzz, but also his friends found all his excitement and enthusiasm infectious. He was a joy to be with.

However, at the moment, he was looking anxious, hardly speaking to his friends (in fact a few of them where getting a little annoyed at the lack of attention he was giving them) and spending all his time sliming about from one practise session to the next.

"Come on, Curly, give yourself a breather, mate. Me and the guys are heading to the blossom tree for a chilled out glass of sap, and watching the sun go down. Fancy joining us?" asked Woodster.

"Love to, mate, but can't stop. Got dirt to burn."

"Curly!" groaned Woodster, watching his snaily friend slide away into the distance while shaking his head.

With the sun setting in the distance, barely visible over the huge garden fence and definitely not noticed by Curly Whirly, the speedy snail prepared himself for another shellblading session.

"Helmet? Check!" confirmed Curly to himself.

"Sweet looking sunglasses? Check," he continued, smiling to himself.

"Right then, let's do this!" And with that he pulled himself inside his shell and started rolling down the track for another hard pushed training session. "I'll show you."

He was now skimming down the track, dust kicking up everywhere and the whistling sound of the air rattling around inside his shell and ears filled him with joy and confidence. He was aware that he was doing well. He was speeding. He was 'in the zone'!

He slowly peered out with one long tentacled eye, knowing that a corner was approaching and he had to get ready to lean to the left, when the feeling of panic gripped his heart hard. It was dark and shadowy outside, he felt a little tired and still had his sunglasses on when he realised, "Oh heck, I can't really see." Wallop!

Suddenly all the air was thumped out of his little foot-like body, he could feel his shell spinning itself and him in a direction he didn't want to go in and on top of that, where were his sunglasses? He then felt a sudden bump to the head, a cracking sound coming from his shell (which didn't sound good) and then blackness engulfed him and pushed him into a kind of direct sleep.

Voices echoed around the inside of his head. His eyes slowly opened. Although they were feeling heavy, he carried on trying to lift them.

"Yo dude, that was rad!" screamed a fellow snail he had seen shellblading before.

"What was?" He felt confused, but slowly the realisation of what had just happened came back to him. "Oh yeah, wow, that was mad," he spluttered with a strange feeling of both joy and pride for surviving.

"Your shell's whack, pest," the other racer snail continued, grinning away to himself as he slowly adjusted his own helmet and moved on.

Curly Whirly quickly looked himself over.

"Shell? Cracked," he groaned.

"Sunglasses? Gone," he groaned again.

"Time? Time for bed," he slowly groaned, picking himself up and gently sliding off the dusty track.

The next morning the now lumpy racer snail slowly got himself out of bed and out into the garden.

His shell wasn't looking good and would need some major renovation work to be ready in time for the race. A horrible dent sat in the middle of his coiled shell like a crater sat on the face of the big, white, cheesy moon found in the sky at night.

"Better find Woodster. He'll knock you back into shape," he said to himself.

"Is the moon made of cheese, Dad?" quizzed a baffled looking Harry.

"Nah, it's just an old tale or fable. Just a silly bit of fun," laughed Dad.

Harry went thoughtful, then continued "If it was made of cheese would people keep going up to it on spaceships and eat it?"

"I doubt it, even though the cheese is nice on the moon apparently there's no atmosphere up there" chuckled Dad to himself.

Harry frowned.

"Anyway, back to the garden and the insect hotel," interjected Dad, trying to get to lights out time sooner rather than later.

"You missed a great sun-down the other night, Curly," moaned Woodster.

"Yeah, sure I did. More fun than smashing myself into dirt and dust, I bet."

"Ha, no doubt about that. Was lovely and peaceful with all sorts of creamy looking reds and orange colours filling the skies," Woodster continued, "cuddled up with huge fluffy pillow like clouds."

Curly Whirly suspected a moan was coming, hidden in the disguise of a friendly chat.

"The sap was top notch as well. Stinker couldn't get enough of it. At one point he had it dripping out of his ears," laughed the hardworking woodlouse as he slowly started to hammer the racing shell back into shape.

"Good old Stinker," replied Curly Whirly.

"Yeah. When was the last time you caught up with us properly anyway?" asked Woodster.

"Erm," pondered the snail, knowing he was now getting lectured for neglecting them.

"Yeah, been a while hasn't it?" Woodster said. "Too busy rushing about, racing and crashing to fit us in, hey?"

"Yeah, I guess. Sorry."

"No trouble, we're always here for you. That's what friends are for, isn't it, slimey? Being there for each other."

Curly Whirly knew he'd not been a great pal recently, so shrugged his shoulders and nodded in acknowledgement thinking it best to take the ear bashing and moan, get it over with and hopefully move on soon.

"Did you get chance to see those mushrooms, near the track, before they got nibbled away?" continued Woodster.

"No, I didn't get chance."

"Shame! Not seen them in the garden for a long time, something lovely and magical about mushrooms in a night garden."

"Yeah," replied the shellblader, admittedly a little disappointed that he had missed them. He'd never seen mushrooms in the garden before, he realised.

"Downside to rushing about, I guess. Miss some of the lovely things that are all around us," said the woodlouse, giving the snail a knowing look and wink. "Anyway, all done now." And with that he passed the snail his racing helmet back.

"On your marks!" shouted the race official, the slight drizzle from the rain catching his safety visor.

"Get set. GO!" And with that all the shellblading snails dived inside their shells and started rolling down the sodden, muddy dirt track as fast as they could.

"Wee hee," squealed Curly Whirly as he started the descent into the first corner, his shell spinning around like a Catherine wheel firework, throwing wet mud high up into the air. Thumping the ground hard and fast behind him was the huge Escargot.

"Here's Escargot," boomed the large snail as he closed in hard on Curly. The mud didn't seem to affect him in any way.

"Ha ha," laughed Curly Whirly, re-discovering the fun of the race. He wasn't really paying any attention to his arch rival's presence or comments as he sailed down the track.

All around the track lined up various insects in various colours, sizes and shapes, cheering on all the racing snails as they belted through the bog-like mud.

It was after clearing the second bend that Curly Whirly slowed slightly to look up at something which had caught his eye. It was a huge curved line of colours coming from the dark, grey looking bags of rain in the sky, down to the ground off in the far distance.

"Wow, will you look at that?" he said in Escargot's direction. "What do you suppose it is?"

Escargot, ignoring him, seized his opportunity to thunder past and overtake the chocolate-coloured shelled snail, who was still slowing and gazing leisurely into the sky. "Later," he yelled, laughing.

Curly Whirly didn't seem to mind. He loved racing and the thrill of it, as well as the taking part, but this vision of strange colour coming from the skies was something that blew him away. "Hope the guys can see this," he thought.

It was then that the next sharp corner approached. It was raised slightly higher than the rest of the track, sandy and pebble filled. In his excitement at overtaking Curly Whirly, Escargot was now hitting at break-shell speed.

"Oh crumbs," the huge snail gasped, as he realised his mistake and hit the side of the track like a bull hitting a shop full of china.

Thud!

"So did Curly Whirly win Dad?" quizzed Harry.

"What do you think? It's up to you."

Harry tilted his head in contemplation. "I think he stopped to help the big snail."

"Wow. That's lovely, Harry. Then that's what he did, he stopped to help him." Dad smiled and ruffled his son's hair and then reached for the light switch.

"But he thrashed him next time," giggled Harry

# 4: Conundrum and Nutmeg

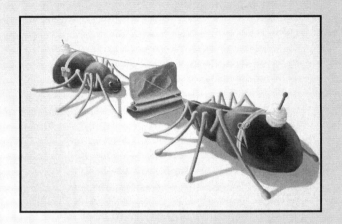

"Come on, Harry. Let's check out the Insect Hotel!" cried out Dad as he stepped into the garden, stretching out his weary arms while at the same time enjoying the blast of fresh air and sunshine that hit him from the great outdoors.

There was something about the birds singing happily in the sun, insects flying about minding their own business and the rustling of the leaves in the trees that always made Dad feel at peace and content with the world. That and a cold beverage!

But as he was strolling peacefully down the garden Dad suddenly became aware of something! Something which suddenly

felt different in the air. Something forceful, something with meaning and something with purpose was fast approaching him from behind. He could feel and hear the thudding vibrations of the ground shake around him, could sense the wildlife nearby go quiet and hold in its breath as he himself looked around in slow anticipation of some unknown force which was descending upon him.

"Nnnnnneeeeeeyyyyyooooooooaaahhhhhhh!" yelled Harry flying past him, running full pelt towards the bottom of the garden with arms outstretched, white scuffed trainers a blur on the ground.

"I win!" Harry cheered jumping up in the air, pleased with his latest victory over Dad.

"Well done, kidder," grinned Dad, ruffling Harry's hair as he caught him up. "Right, let's see what we've got here," he said as he crouched down to have a closer look at the Insect Hotel, with the air of someone who knew what they were doing.

Harry (watching his dad carefully) copied his dad's crouching down position, hand on chin and thoughtful, peering look towards the hotel. Little gnats flew about, some ants could be seen rushing about in various directions and a local hoverfly suspiciously watched them from a distance.

"Someone's been busy, " said Dad.

Harry looked at him curiously.

Pointing towards the first floor of the hotel Dad said, "Look, can you see all the little bits of web everywhere?"

Harry nodded.

"Looks like the spiders staying over have started redecorating our hotel. There's long webs draped all over the first floor and some more tucked around the back."

Then as they both stood up in unison, Dad asked with a smile, "Did you say they could?"

"Nope," Harry quickly replied.

"Cheeky things. Me neither. Fancy not liking my decorating skills."

"So your bedroom then, Harry. We decided on a pirate or dinosaur theme?" asked Dad as he switched off the bedroom light.

"Pirate!" shouted Harry.

Then before Dad reached the door, he asked, "Why did the spiders decorate the hotel?"

"No, No, No!" shrieked Nutmeg at the top of his high pitched voice. He covered his wide open mouth with his silk wrapped two front feet, his big set of eyes almost popping out of his head with the brown tinge of colour there appearing to turn red like fire. For a spider, he was good looking – nice shiny black coat, long slender but powerfully built legs and a mischievous smile other spiders found hard not to like. In fact many thought him dashing, especially with the air of confidence he always conveyed.

Conundrum span round, looking at his long term friend in disgust not only at startling him a little by shouting out, not only for starting to cause a scene, but mainly for becoming the centre of attention to all the other insects swarming around the hotel lobby.

"What now?" replied Conundrum as he flounced over in a bit of a huff, adjusting his rather elaborate looking flat cap on his head, which he had fashioned himself from many different, light coloured materials. Like his friend Nutmeg, Conundrum was quite dashing, always wearing the latest style of clothes, always had slight splashes of silver colour sprinkled into his thick black and spiky hair, which he believed made him look more resplendent.

"This place," said Nutmeg.

"What, what about it. It's quaint!"

Nutmeg glared at his friend in a very dramatic manner as he became aware that all insects in the lobby hotel had now stopped to look at them both.

"Quaint?" he asked. "Quaint? Oh no, don't you dare!"

Conundrum glared back. He'd picked the hotel, so knew it wasn't going to be good enough no matter what it looked like. On top of that, as they were both now in front of a stunned and curious crowd of bugs, he was not about to back down in this little verbal boxing match. "Let the performance begin," he thought.

Nutmeg continued, "Red brick! I ask you, red brick with brown wooden flooring?" pointing at both the floor and the walls with his long silk clad middle legs, front legs now going back to covering his mouth and face which had gone back into a look of shock.

"Oh please!" dismissed Conundrum, as he walked back to the reception desk. "It's called rustic. All top hotels are going that way."

Nutmeg glared again at his friend, looking like he'd been slapped in the face with a wet tadpole. "Rustic! Rustic! Don't you go flouncing around here dropping terms like quaint and rustic at me!"

Conundrum stopped still and slowly turned back round, smugly smiling at having his friend rattled in this strange argument, this strange battle of mind chess. The rest of the insect guests, now looking around the hotel themselves started thinking or discussing quietly amongst themselves the good or bad look of 'rustic' and did they like quaint or not?

Both spiders were now in full flow, loving the argument, loving the 'one-up spidermanship' and more importantly loving the attention from all the insect guests that had swarmed around them.

"The style in these hard times, my friend, is for the simple, is for the basics," said Connundrum, and then with determined feeling, as he could feel the crowds intake of breath, he added, "for the RUSTIC!"

Some of the crowd gave out a little cheer, some gasped and some started to edge towards Conundrum, until Nutmeg rose up and gave them a distasteful stare.

"Some insects still feel they deserve a little comfort and style. I deserve some comfort after my gruelling work load and travel commitments lately!" Nutmeg then paused for effect, head raised at an angle and secretly glancing at the crowd that had formed in the lobby. "The style, well... I have cobwebs full of that!" he spat.

Conundrum smiled. Nutmeg could play a crowd, and how could he deny his friend some comfort? And if he continued this verbal tug-of-war, well, their holiday break would be ruined by

constant whinging and sulking. The 'cobwebs full of style' comment? Well, he wasn't so sure about that.

After the scene in the lobby the hotel staff keenly moved both spiders into the newly built penthouse suite, located in the newly built roof, which was so brand spankingly new you could still hear the echoes of Woodster's hammerings reverberating around the walls.

Nutmeg and Conundrum looked around the room. It was spacious, untouched and a tad... minimalistic (Empty). Any hard working and honest estate agent would have happily claimed the same.

However, neither of the spiders this time was overly impressed. One of the dandy spiders then turned and menacingly raised himself up over the poor little ant bellhop, who had escorted them and their luggage upstairs; his eyes now wide open as he nervously adjusted his red hat, realising he had no chance of a piece of crumb (tip) today. "Nice room, little fella, but tell me, who did you have in to furnish this place?"

The little bellhop just stared blankly at him.

"Thought so!" yelled Nutmeg from the other side of the room.

"Looks like we came just in time." Conundrum smiled at the bellhop. "You can go now."

And with that he dismissed the ant from the room with a flick of two of his middle feet.

"Did the spiders not like the comfy straw and sticks we put in then, Dad?" enquired Harry with a hint of disappointment.

"Doesn't sound like it, does it?"

"Why not, what would they have wanted?"

"Most spiders wouldn't mind the furnishings we used, it's just Conundrum and Nutmeg have... different tastes. Think they just want things their way!" Dad replied.

"Lots of webs?"

"Yep," shrugged Dad.

"Are they being naughty?"

Dad hesitated and then replied, "No, not really, they just like what they like. Probably just want everyone to like what they like, too."

"Yes, I agree, rustic is beautiful and helps this place with its... character, but I do strongly feel as I'm sure you do yourself, this places needs a little bit more..." And with that, arms moving in circles, Conundrum went thoughtful, searching for the right word to share with the hotel's lobby manager.

"Style," interjected Nutmeg with a knowing smile.

Conundrum and the lobby manager both looked at Nutmeg.

Conundrum nodded. "My friend here is right, of course, but it needs a little..." and again he paused still searching for the correct word that he was hoping would convince the manager to give him and Nutmeg the go-ahead to start a redecorating project and perhaps even earn them some crumbs on the side.

"Softening," he blurted out finally, pleased to have found what he felt was an appropriate word for the plans he had to change the hotel lobby look.

He then peered at the lobby manager, who was clearly over-whelmed by both the spider's passion and forcefulness to add some 'softening' to his lobby.

"Fine," he stammered, hoping this would mean the spiders would go away, that he would get left alone. It would also give him the chance to have a much needed sip of sap.

Suddenly the normally peaceful and organised lobby was filled with step ladders, webbing, tubs of glue and splatterings of mayhem as both spiders set to work on adding some 'softening' to the hotel.

The hotel staff and guests were soon getting accustomed to the shouting, screaming and extravagant tantrums which had become commonplace in the reception and lobby area. Both Nutmeg and Conundrum went from one apparent disaster to the next in what seemed to the bewildered insects passing by simply a decorating job of putting curtains up.

 "Ha, what do they know?" squealed Nutmeg, looking down at them with disgust.

A couple of days into the 'softening' of the hotel lobby, the cool morning winds blowing freshness into every nook and cranny found in the garden, Stinker and Woodster headed towards the hotel. "Not sure this bow tie really goes with my builder's apron, Stinker," grumbled Woodster, as they both headed through the big hotel entrance doors.

 Then suddenly, wham! Both Stinker and Woodster found themselves squashed far too closely together, along with some of

the other bugs in the lobby, to be even remotely classed as being comfortable.

"What in the name of the garden is going on here?" grumbled Woodster. "Are we all auditioning for parts in a sardine can?"

"What can I say? The silk webbing is too special to be touched, so everyone including staff have to keep a distance from it," replied the harassed looking reception ant, red uniform hat tilted at an angle and almost falling off.

"But there's no room for any bug to move around or breathe," commented Stinker, suddenly aware that the runner bean juice was starting to bubble up inside him, making him panic a little bit as now would definitely not be a good time to have an incident.

"It's hardly a relaxing environment for us all, now is it?" added Woodster, looking around the confined lobby area as little gnats and ants where forced to clamber over one another to get in or out of the hotel.

"I like style as much as the next bug," said Stinker, adjusting his bright yellow bow tie as if this garment further proved his point, "but I think it's time you cut back on the old silk webbing! It's everywhere."

In hearing this comment a few nearby, frazzled and stressed looking lobby guests squeaked a little, "Hear, hear!" as they where bundled, foot in face, in a direction they didn't really want to go in.

"The cheek of it," snapped Nutmeg, dragging his suitcase behind him in a form of protest, which no-one else seemed to notice or get.

"Questioning our work, our style and our ideas!" he continued. "Conundrum! Get me out of here."

Conundrum followed behind, looking at the lobby area which was now full to the brim with extravagant silk webbed curtains that gave off a lovely hint of comfort and class (he felt). He sighed, with his front leg held dramatically across his chest. "Oh, departure is such sweet sorrow."

"Humph," replied Nutmeg, who was still reeling from the hotel staff asking whether it would be okay to take down some of the silk webbing from the hotel.

"Complaints? I have a complaint. The insects here all BUG me." And with that he stomped out of the door in a very sulky manner, his friend following slowly behind him.

"Where to now, then?" pondered Nutmeg once outside.

"Somewhere further afield? Perhaps deep in the country?" replied Conundrum.

"I've got it!" yelled Nutmeg excitedly. "Grass Vegas! Let's go see all the lights and sun dew."

Conundrum gave a thoughtful, positive nod as he processed the idea.

"Besides," said Nutmet, "this place has got a bit dull. I mean look at it, way too much silk webbing for my liking."

"I suppose," sighed Conundrum. "You can have too much of a good thing." And with that, they both jumped off the lobby front porch down into the deep lush grasses of the garden below.

Minutes later some of the guests, sitting and relaxing on deck chairs, looking out at the lovely and colourful views of the garden, could hear the strange spider friends bickering in the undergrowth as they debated the benefits of leopard skin suitcases.

"Dad, do you think the spiders will come back to the insect hotel?"

"Hope so, son," replied Dad, getting up to leave the bedroom.

"Why?" yawned Harry.

"Well, someone needs to help clean up all those webs left lying around, don't they?"

With that Harry smiled and started to roll over.

"Tourists, hey!" grinned Dad as he left the room.

# 5: Gamble

Gamble was a ladybird. He had a hard wearing but nice, shiny red coat with black spots. He always donned a straw hat, could always be found holding a trowel and was always moaning about the temperature being too cold. Gamble worked in the garden as a park warden, a cross between a gardener and a security guard for all the different flowers and plants he helped grow and later to bloom.

Gamble got his name, jokingly, after from his point of view a rather rough game of Roulette which involved some big frogs throwing him around like a dice, which unfortunately for Gamble lasted quite a while. The frogs (not being too bright) didn't realise the number of dots on his back always stayed the same, so lucky (unlucky for Gamble) number seven kept repeating over and over again the more they threw him. This pleased the frogs no end. Gamble however wasn't as pleased and was also a strange looking black and blue coloured ladybird for quite a while after.

Strangely enough from then on Gamble always avoided frogs, as well as spiders that mocked and teased him for what happened.

"Shouldn't have mentioned having a barbecue today, hey, Harry?" grumbled Dad, looking up at the darkening sky, as clouds formed over head like a mass of hungry, dark and grumpy sheep about to descend upon an uncut field.

Harry looked up as well, however he had waited far too long and was far too hungry with the idea of having a tasty burger (with sauce) to want Dad to stop now. "It's okay, Dad."

Dad didn't seem to listen or believe him, so Harry looked around, saw his big yellow slide and decided to climb around on that instead. "I know." thought Harry. "If I climb to the top of the slide and shout at Dad that it's okay for a Bar-B-Q, he'll still do it." And up he went.

Meanwhile, Gamble was feeling the chill. He had chased away some naughty looking greenflies who liked to make a mess of his veggie patch and was heading back to the hotel to settle down, hopefully before the clouds split and let water come flooding down upon the garden.

"Were you spotted?" sniggered some spiders, emphasising the word 'spotted' and giggling to each other about their own comedy genius.

Gamble groaned to himself, quickly looked around to see if he could find a different way back in order to avoid these two nuisances and further torment. He couldn't. The only other option involved flying close to a huge yellow plastic mountain (Harry's slide) which was known to sometimes contain a very loud monkey creature which had no fear of falling from great heights while squealing in pleasure.

"Just ignore them, Gamble," he said to himself as he got closer, and continued his direct path back to the hotel.

"Ladybird, Ladybird, fly away home," the spiders started singing with a sound similar to that of chalk scraping across a blackboard. "Coz the frogs are out playing, and calling your name," they sniggered loudly.

Gamble was now starting to grind his antenna in frustration and flap his little wings harder. "Why don't you both just shut up and leave me alone!" he screamed.

"Oooooohhhhh" the spiders mocked, now holding onto each other with laughter, pleased with getting a reaction from Gamble.

"Aaaggghhhh," yelled Gamble and quickly spun around to change direction, heading straight for the big yellow mountain of monkey screams.

"Is it ready now, Dad?" shouted Harry from the top of his slide.

"Not yet, not even got the fire going yet," shrugged Dad and looked up at the clouds as they gathered above. "Hope we can beat that rain."

The wind was slowly starting to pick up, causing the blossom tree to lean over slightly and rustle in protest. Something then caught Harry's eye, something flying straight for him, something little and something fast.

"Gotcha," he yelled as he cupped the little bug in both hands.

"What you got?" Dad asked Harry without looking away from the very demanding job of poking the barbecue coal and fire with a fork like utensil, concentration wiped across his face

as he carefully moved coals around, as if playing a game of chess against the wind.

Harry peered into his hands. "Ladybird, Ladybird, I've got a Ladybird!" he sang out loud, feeling very proud of his accomplishment, as he started climbing down from the slide.

"Look, Dad, Look," he said as he pushed his hands towards his dad.

"Careful, mind the barbecue, it's getting hot!" panicked Dad as Harry came bursting towards him – and the very small fire – like a boulder tumbling down a mountainside.

"Why's it called a Ladybird if it's not a bird?" asked Harry.

"Oh crumbs," thought Gamble, now prisoner in a huge, sticky and strangely sweet smelling pair of hands. He quickly looked around for some small glimpse of an escape route, but found this a difficult task. He continually felt a little disorientated or like he was flying, though he wasn't moving.

Suddenly the cavernous prison which had engulfed him opened up and he looked up to see a huge face peering at him. It was bigger than the monkey creature which had captured him but nevertheless just as strange looking. Gripped with fear, Gamble chose not to move. "I know, I'll play dead," he thought and stayed perfectly still.

"It worked," he thought as the prison hands of stickiness closed up around him again. "The big thing hasn't eaten me," and suddenly he was aware that he was on the move again.

A few minutes later, in one of the most bumpy journeys Gamble could recall, the prison hands opened up again and he could feel lovely fresh air hitting him as he suddenly felt himself sliding downwards, out of the prison.

Bump. Landing was a little harder than he would of liked, but was worth it to escape the strangely 'sweetie' smelling dungeon he had just resided in. Looking around he suddenly felt overcome with joy. "I'm back!" he cheered, as he found himself back at the Insect Hotel lobby.

"You one lucky bug, Gamble," commented Woodster, perched on a twig inside the hotel bar slowly finishing off a sip of sap.

"I suppose, although I still can't get this stickiness of my shell!"

"Why you flew so close to that yellow mountain of monkeys I'll never know!" said Woodster, as he tried to get the waiter's attention in order to get another drink.

"Was either that or listen to those dandy spiders laugh at me again," Gamble grumbled.

"Spiders laugh at you? So what, rather that then become a giant monkeys book mark."

"Book mark?"

"Look, Gamble, stop letting them spiders or any other insect upset you or wind you up so easily! You can't let others affect what you want to do or where you want to go. Life's too short."

"I know, but..."

"But nothing! Two spiders who you don't really like or care for nearly got you squished or something today," pointed out Woodster, who was both getting annoyed by what had happened and feeling sorry for his friend.

Gamble went thoughtful. He knew his friend was right, and he didn't like getting so hurt or upset by others but, well, what could he do?

"Look, my friend, either learn to ignore them or find another way to handle it. There is always going to be some bug out there who is going to try and wind you up or have fun with you."

"I've tried ignoring it," Gamble said limply.

"Then let's try something else. Want to know what I do?"

"You? Who teases you? Everyone just has a laugh with you," quizzed the ladybird. "Or avoids you."

"That's my trick, buddy. When some bug says something to annoy, hurt or tease me... I laugh along with it, or make a joke myself about it!"

"Hey?"

"Yep, they soon stop if they know their words aren't hurting me, because I'm laughing at the same words or adding to them. Takes the sting out of it!"

Gamble nodded thoughtfully.

"Just don't take yourself or others so seriously. You'll find the name calling soon stops if it's not having the effect they want. Now, where's that work-shy waiter with my drink?" moaned Woodster as he clambered up the twig to search for more sap.

A few days had passed since his chat with Woodster, and Gamble had spent that time contemplating his friend's words, as well as keeping a check on the veggie patch and that everything was growing lovely.

"Right then," he muttered to himself. "Let's do this," and off he buzzed in the direction where he last saw the two mocking spiders.

Again, it was cool breezy day with the sun trying its best to peek around the shoulders of the big, white fluffy clouds. Gamble, adjusting his new 'book design' bow tie Stinker had sold him, took in a deep breath and headed 'full on' to where he had spied the two spiders.

"Ay up, spotty, how's it rolling?" one of them chuckled as they noticed the ladybird fly by.

"Hello, you two, how's you?"

That baffled the teasing spiders for a moment as they looked at each other, both wearing matching blue baseball caps and bright white T-shirts with 'Broken Web? Darn it!' written on them. But they quickly shook their heads, as if trying to clear them, snapped out of their surprised state and continued with their wind ups "Erm, we're fine! So, what's a lovely lady like you doing in a garden like this?"

"Lady? Come on, guys, you can do better that that," Gamble laughed back. "I've heard that a million times, besides... I'm too ugly to be a lady!" And with that both spiders laughed.

"He sure is," the smaller of the two giggled. Then both stopped suddenly, looked at each other again with mouths and eyes wide open as they realised, Gamble had come out with the joke and put down.

Sensing the confusion of the spiders, and secretly enjoying himself, Gamble continued, "Anyway, lads, as much fun as this has been, I gotta go," and with that started to head off in the direction of the hotel.

The smaller of the two spiders started to panic, stuttering in his attempt to quickly find another one liner to upset the almost smug-looking ladybird as he started to depart. "Yeah… I well… erm, what about the frogs!" he spat.

"What about them?" replied Gamble, stopping slowly and looking over his shoulder as casually as he could, hoping the next comment wouldn't be too nasty or get a reaction from him.

"Erm… I hear they're hungry and fancy a SPOT of tea," the spider spluttered out, more in relief that he could think of another kind of put down than anything else. His colleague just looked at him, a little disappointed with his friend's poor attempt at a jibe.

"Think I'll leave it and catch them another time. Besides, don't think it's tea they like. I hear they prefer a cup of hot Croak-o!"

(Narrator apologises for poor joke!)

Both spiders again looked at each other. What was going on?

"Maybe we should all drop by the pool sometime, see if the frogs fancy a quick game of spin the spider or something like that." Gamble winked over at them both.

"Yeah, sounds... good," the bigger of the two replied, as he realised with gaping mouth that this game would involve him being skimmed hard across the top of the pond. He peered at his friend, who just looked blankly at him, and gulped.

"Later then, crawlers." And with that Gamble sped off, pleased with himself for not getting upset or reacting. "Seems Woodster was right after all," he thought.

Both spiders then looked at each other, wondering what on earth had happened there? The bigger of the two then cuffed the little one on the shoulder. "Numpty! What kind of a joke was that?" he blurted out and then in a mocking voice said, "I hear the frogs want a spot of tea," and shook his head in disgust.

"Sorry, best I could think of."

"Well, don't think any more. Your jokes are mud."

"He seemed all right though, didn't he?" muttered the little spider, looking at the ground despondently.

"Yeah, not a bad little ladybird after all."

# How we made our Insect Hotel

I've always been a nature lover and enjoyed spending time out-doors, enthralled with the beauty of every little thing nature offers us, from the birds and the bees to all other insect types, which aren't always popular with everyone.

Insects not only help both flowers and plants pollinate, but they also attract other wildlife like birds into our gardens. I en-joy and encourage the regular visits of some Blue Tits into my garden, with fat balls and nuts already, but was keen to attract others types of birds.

For these reasons, as well as wanting to create an activity both my son and I could do (with no extra cost) decided to at-tempt to build an insect hotel.

So together we went rummaging around both our shed and garden for any bits of wood or material we could find and pos-sibly use. For starters we found a broken and discarded old set of draws and some shelves which we no longer used; these became the base/floors of the hotel.

The foundations (or walls – I'm just trying to sound like I know what I'm doing) came from some bricks I found and have

had lying around the place for years. (Glad I never threw them away now.) The pleasing thing was I found the red bricks with the big holes in! Perfect I think for letting new guests crawl in and out.

So, with the base put down (broken draw) I placed the red bricks around the sides like walls. Then filled that level with lots of broken bamboo sticks (from an old fence panel) I had hidden behind the shed. The holes in the bamboo I believe can be used by little insects to crawl in, nest and lay eggs. I've also seen 'bee homes' in garden centres filled with big bamboo sticks... so if good enough for them, good enough for me.

Once that level/floor was filled, Harry and I plonked two old shelf panels across the top and, as before, around the sides placed more bricks. To be honest, on our hotel, we ran out of the really good red bricks mentioned, so we then had to switch to some smaller blue ones we found. But with these being smaller, we left slight gaps in between to allow easy access to our new guests to enter.

We then filled the second floor: half with straw that I found in the shed and the other half with dry leaves and bark swept up from around the garden. Both these offerings I believe offer guests hibernation materials and, for some, midnight snacks.

Unfortunately we ran out of bricks at this point, but we do have future plan to construct/extend a third floor which we will fill with lots of gathered twigs, sticks and logs.

For decoration we placed a broken plant pot nearby (created by a game of football – oops) which has now resulted in a nice damp little shelter for some slugs. We've also used a big old dead log next to the hotel; think we called this a bridge!

Anyway, hope you'll agree all the above sounds do-able, easy and cheap. We had bags of fun doing this! Hope you'll give it a try, encourage wildlife into your garden and if so, get in touch with us.

# Future adventures

With the fun adventures, discoveries and new friends we have had so far, both Harry and I plan to do more in our garden. Should this book be of interest and enjoyment to people then a second book could be on its way. Below are some of the plans the insect hotel management team have for further expansion.

Birds' nest – For the two regular Blue Tit visitors to our garden

Hedgehog shed – Plans for an extension at the back of the hotel to accommodate hedgehogs

Swimming pool – The pond in the garden to be cleaned up so the frog 'life guards' can run swimming lessons better

Some research into accommodating a grey squirrel that visits (and pinches the bird's nuts) from our garden recently. A definite cheeky chappy.

And hopefully many more friends will further come in and be discovered too.


Thank you.

David S

27409066R00048

Printed in Great Britain
by Amazon